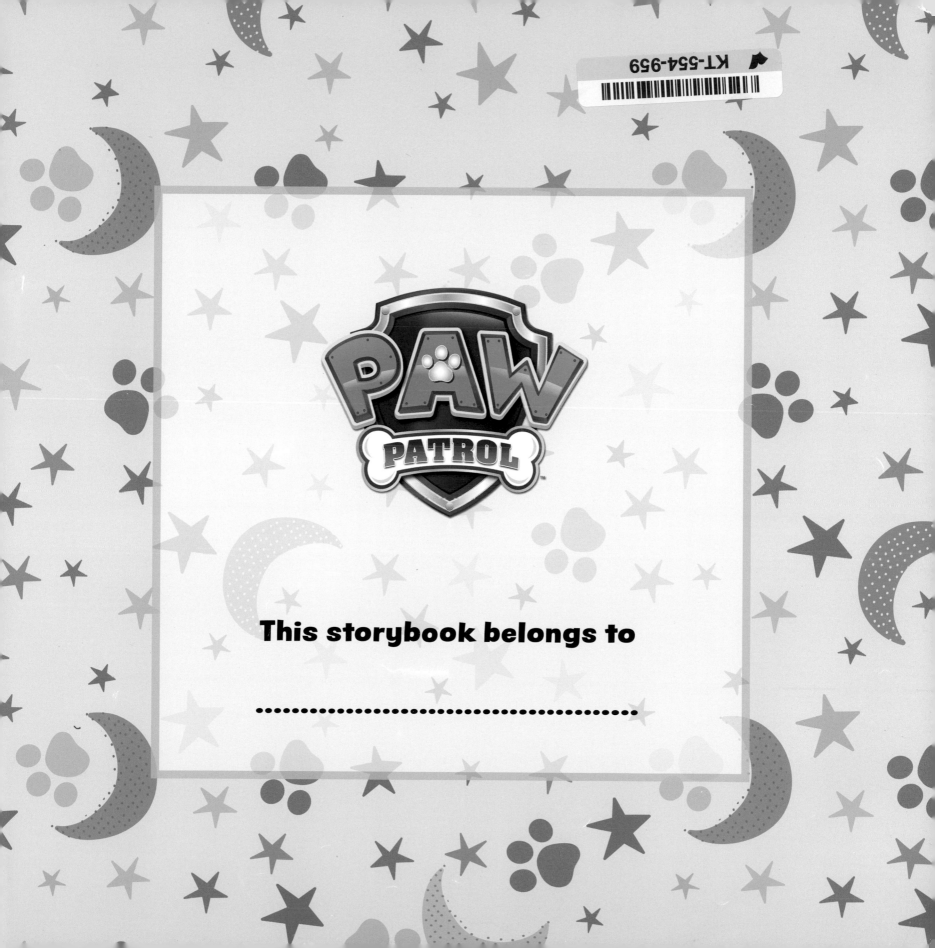

PAW PATROL

This storybook belongs to

....

Farshore

First published in United States 2020 by Penguin Random House
This edition published in Great Britain 2021 by Farshore

An imprint of HarperCollins*Publishers*
1 London Bridge Street, London SE1 9GF
www.farshore.co.uk

HarperCollins*Publishers*
1st Floor, Watermarque Building, Ringsend Road
Dublin 4, Ireland

ISBN 978 0 7555 0267 7
Printed in the United Kingdom
1

Farshore takes its responsibility to the planet and its inhabitants very seriously.
We aim to use papers from well-managed forests run by responsible suppliers.

SNUGGLE UP, PUPS

The stars were out, the moon was full, and everyone in and around Adventure Bay was getting ready for bed. Outside the Town Hall, Chase was helping folks get home safely . . . even Mayor Goodway and Chickaletta!

On the farm, Rubble and Skye were helping Farmer Yumi and Farmer Al finish up their chores. **"Time to hit the hay,"** Farmer Al said with a chuckle.

On the way back to the Lookout, Rubble **slipped** in the mud. **Oops!**

Time to get nice and clean again!

"Rub-a-dub-dub, I sure love the tub!" he sang. "It's the best part of getting ready for bed."

Across town at the Porters' house, Alex was getting ready for bed, too. "The PAW Patrol taught me that brushing keeps my teeth **healthy** and **clean**!" he told his grandad.

Up on Jake's mountain, Everest **crawled** under her blanket. She said good night to the penguins and to her pal Jake.

Out in the jungle, Tracker got cosy on his bed.
He said **buenos noches** to the parrots and to his amigo Carlos.

At the Lookout, Ryder changed into his favourite pyjamas. He let out a big yawn. **"PAW Patrol, let's roll . . . to bed."**

Everyone was **clean** and **cosy**. It was time for a story.
The pups chose a book and gathered around Ryder
so he could read to them.

Skye took a turn **reading** to the pups, too.

Marshall gave his teddy a **big hug**.

While Rubble setttled down to **sleep**.

Everest **snuggled up**, high on the mountain . . .

And Rocky was cosy under his **soft blanket**.

Sleep tight and turn out the lights.

It's time to **snuggle up, pups!**

THE END

AN ACTION-PACKED VOLCANO ADVENTURE

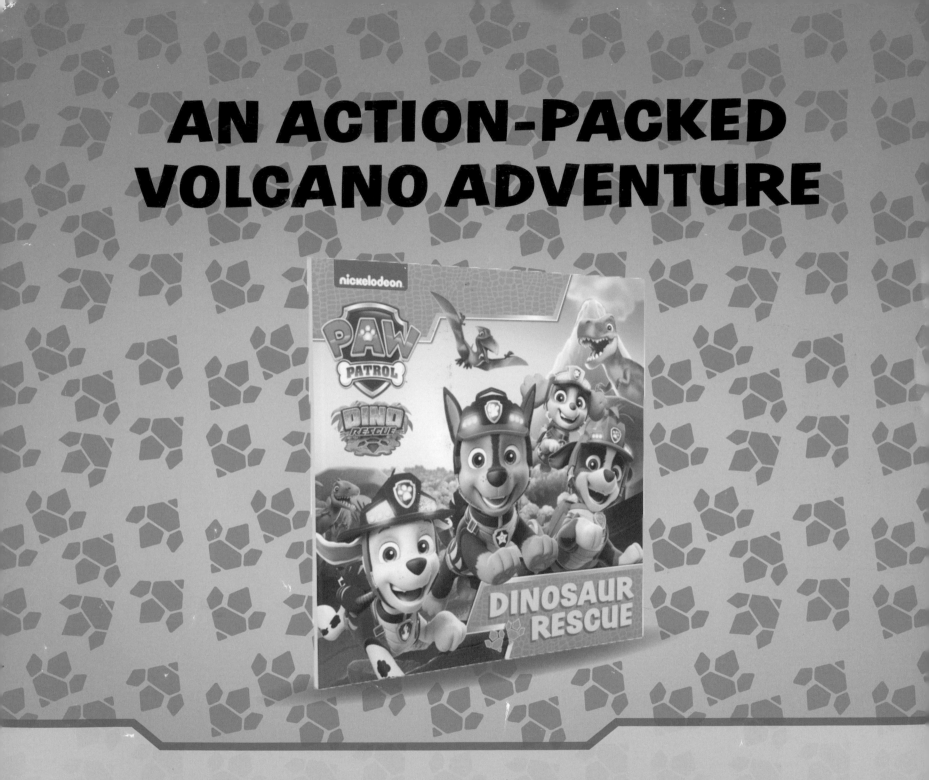

ROAR! When some dinosaur friends are in need the PAW Patrol gang are ready to help. It's all hands on deck to help save the dinosaurs from a huge volcano.

ISBN: 9780755502660